TIP-OFF
BASKETBALL

SMALL
FORWARD

By Jason Glaser

Must
Read!

Gareth Stevens
Publishing

Please visit our Web site, www.garethstevens.com. For a free color catalog of all our high-quality books, call toll free 1-800-542-2595 or fax 1-877-542-2596.

Library of Congress Cataloging-in-Publication Data

Glaser, Jason.
Small forward / Jason Glaser.
     p. cm. — (Tip-off, basketball)
ISBN 978-1-4339-3984-6 (pbk.)
ISBN 978-1-4339-3985-3 (6 pack)
ISBN 978-1-4339-3983-9 (library binding)
1. Forwards (Basketball) I. Title.
GV885.G57 2011
796.323 B—dc22

                          2010012454

First Edition

Published in 2011 by
Gareth Stevens Publishing
111 East 14th Street, Suite 349
New York, NY 10003

Copyright © 2011 Gareth Stevens Publishing

Designer: Michael J. Flynn
Editor: Greg Roza

Gareth Stevens Publishing would like to thank consultant Stephen Hayn, men's basketball coach at Dowling College, for his guidance in writing this book.

Photo credits: Cover, p. 1 Kevork Djansezian/Getty Images; cover, back cover, pp. 2–3, 5, 7, 11, 17, 21, 25, 29, 31, 35, 43–48 (basketball court background on all), 9, 19, 26, 30, 33, 42, 43 (basketball border on all) Shutterstock.com; p. 4 Manny Millan/Sports Illustrated/Getty Images; p. 5 Dick Raphael/ Sports Illustrated/Getty Images; p. 6 George Eastman House/Hulton Archive/Getty Images; pp. 8, 13 Dick Raphael/NBAE/Getty Images; p. 10 NBA Photos/NBAE/Getty Images; p. 11 NBA Classic/NBAE/ Getty Images; p. 12 Neil Leifer/NBAE/Getty Images; p. 14 (James Worthy) Mike Powell/Getty Images; p. 14 (Scottie Pippen) Jonathan Daniel/Getty Images; p. 15 Rick Stewart/Getty Images; p. 18 Chris Graythen/Getty Images; p. 19 Domenic Centofanti/Getty Images; p. 20 Wen Roberts/ NBAE/Getty Images; pp. 21, 31 Ron Tureene/NBAE/Getty Images; p. 22 Rocky Widner/NBAE/ Getty Images; p. 23 David Sherman/NBAE/Getty Images; p. 24 Cameron Browne/NBAE/ Getty Images; p. 25 Garrett Ellwood/NBAE/Getty Images; p. 26 Lou Capozzola/Sports Illustrated/ Getty Images; pp. 27, 35 Doug Pensinger/Getty Images; p. 28 Kent Smith/NBAE/Getty Images; p. 29 Jesse D. Garrabrant/NBAE/Getty Images; p. 30 Stephen Dunn/Getty Images; p. 32 Lisa Blumfeld/ Getty Images; p. 33 Sam Greenwood/Getty Images; p. 34 Ezra Shaw/Getty Images; pp. 36, 37 Elsa/Getty Images; p. 38 Ronald Martinez/Getty Images; p. 39 Ron Hoskins/NBAE/Getty Images; p. 41 Ray Pietro/ Photonica/Getty Images; p. 42 Rana Faure/Riser/Getty Images; p. 43 Inti St. Clair/Digital Vision/Getty Images; p. 44 Kevin C. Cox/Getty Images; p. 45 Robert Laberge/Getty Images.

Printed in the United States of America

CPSIA compliance information: Batch #CS10GS: For further information contact Gareth Stevens, New York, New York at 1-800-542-2595.

CONTENTS

Boldface words appear in the glossary.

The Playmakers

The small forward is the player who must do everything well on offense. The team also counts on him to make big plays on defense.

Winners Want the Ball

In 1987, the Boston Celtics faced the Detroit Pistons in the playoffs. Each team had won two games, and Detroit was close to winning a third. The Pistons led 108–107 with very little time left. However, Boston had the ball. Small forward Larry Bird tried to shoot a game-winning basket but it was blocked. Bird's teammate went for the ball but knocked it out of bounds.

Boston Celtic Larry Bird protects the ball from Detroit Piston Adrian Dantley during the 1987 playoffs.

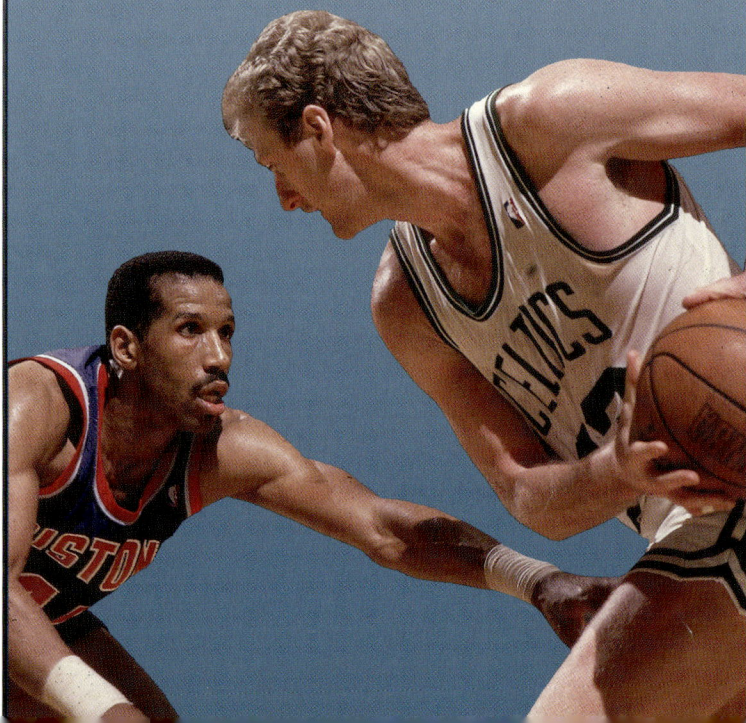

4

Larry Bird celebrates with teammate Dennis Johnson after beating the Detroit Pistons.

Amazing Comeback

With just 5 seconds left, all Detroit needed to do was pass the ball in bounds and hold it. The Detroit player passed the ball in, but Bird zipped across the court and **intercepted** it. He kept his balance at the **baseline** long enough to pass to his teammate, who scored with 1 second left. Boston won the game 109–108!

5

Moving Forward

The forward position in basketball has always been an exciting one to play. The pace and speed of the forward's game have only increased over the years.

Running the Offense

A basketball team in 1891 used nine players with three forwards on offense. Their job was to score by getting the ball into a peach basket hung on the wall. Forwards stayed near their basket, with one forward right below it. They only played defense when the other team got the ball back on a **turnover**.

Even though the first basketball games were played in gyms, it quickly became a popular outdoor sport.

A Dangerous Game

Having players right under the basket often ended in rough play and **fouls** as players fought for the ball. Teams quickly changed to using five players with two forwards, one on each side of the basket. Fewer players were fighting for the ball, even though it could still get wild under the basket.

early basketball positions

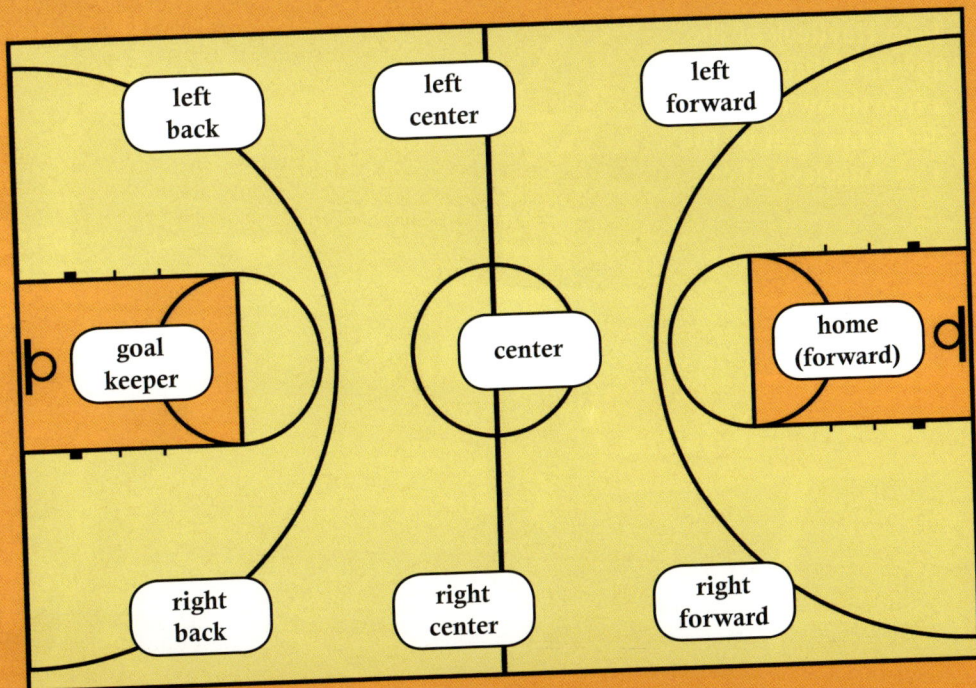

left back	left center	left forward
goal keeper	center	home (forward)
right back	right center	right forward

Players also had to control themselves so they didn't commit fouls. Illegal contact between players resulted in a **free throw** for the player who was fouled. Years ago, players who had committed too many fouls had to leave the game for a half or until the other team scored. Today, an **NBA** player who's committed six fouls must sit out the rest of the game!

John Havlicek of the Boston Celtics shoots a free throw during a 1969 game against the Los Angeles Lakers.

free-throw lane

8

free-throw lane

Many officials felt the game was still too rough under the baskets. They added a rule to keep too many players from being there. It said an offensive player could only stand in the **free-throw lane** for 3 seconds unless his team takes a shot on basket. Today, offensive players move in and out of this area quickly while waiting for a pass.

Playing in the Paint

The free-throw lane is a rectangle marked by four lines underneath each basket. It's often a different color from the rest of the court to help players know when they're in the lane. For this reason, that area is often called "the paint." Small forwards need to be great players "in the paint."

9

The Best in History

Small forward is perhaps the most challenging position in basketball. Here are some superstars who rose to that challenge.

The Inventor

As a teenager growing up in Philadelphia, Pennsylvania, Paul Arizin sometimes played on courts that doubled as dance floors. They were so slippery that Arizin was off balance when shooting. He began jumping up to shoot more accurately. Arizin took his "jump shot" to the Philadelphia Warriors, where he became one of the leading scorers in the NBA. Today, everyone uses the jump shot.

Arizin's jump shot helped him lead the league in points for the 1951–1952 and 1956–1957 seasons.

The Granny Shot

Part of Barry's strange style was throwing free throws underhanded, which is sometimes called a "granny shot." With it, Barry was one of the most accurate free throwers ever. One season, he nailed 160 of 169 free throws!

A Style All His Own

Only one person has led the **NCAA**, NBA, and **ABA** in scoring. Rick Barry's unusual style brought him that honor. Barry used amazing speed and strength to score points up close. It took years in the pros for him to develop an outside shot. From 1965 to 1980, he went from team to team and league to league, scoring over 25,000 career points.

During the 1978–1979 season, Barry missed only nine free throws! He finished the season with a 0.947 percent free-throw average.

Dr. J

Julius Erving put the "slam" in "slam **dunk**." The man called "the Doctor" flew above other players to score, **rebound**, and block shots. He was the leader in scoring 3 of his 5 years in the ABA during the 1970s. He scored from everywhere, including once from behind the backboard in a playoff game. He put up over 30,000 points in his career—one of the highest totals ever.

Bird for Three!

The three-point line is an arc 23 feet, 9 inches (7.3 m) from the basket. The line is 22 feet (6.7 m) from the basket at the corners. A "field goal," or a basket scored, made from behind this line is worth three points. Larry Bird made 649 three-pointers during his career for a total of 1,947 points.

three-point line

Celtic Legend

The Boston Celtics' Larry Bird could win any number of ways. He might use crafty defense to stop **opponents**. He might nail key three-pointers in the fourth quarter. He also averaged over 24 points a game from 1979 to 1992. Bird scored 59 **triple-doubles** during his career, which places him fifth among all players. In the playoffs, Bird brought his game to a new level. He helped his team win three championships. From 1984 to 1986, he was the NBA's Most Valuable Player (MVP).

"Bird for three" became a popular phrase among Celtic fans during the 1980s.

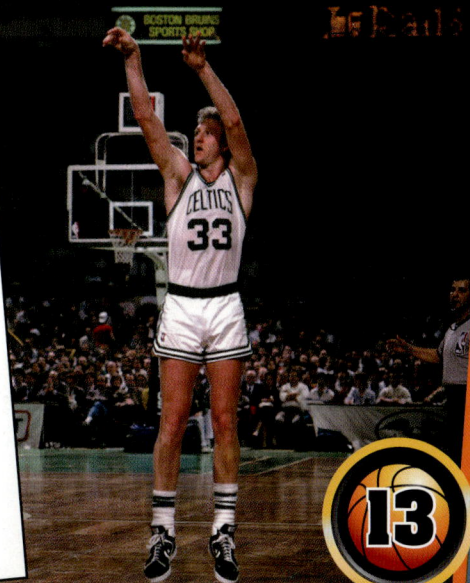

Big Game James

James Worthy was not the biggest player or biggest name on the Los Angeles Lakers, but he could play in the biggest games as well as anyone. "Big Game James" helped his team win three championships in the 1980s. Worthy was the rare player whose numbers got better during the playoffs. He averaged more points and rebounds during the playoffs than during the regular season.

James Worthy

Playoff Wizard

Scottie Pippen was one of the NBA's best defensemen. In 17 seasons between 1987 and 2004, Pippen helped his team reach the playoffs 16 times and win six championships. He averaged two **steals** a game for his entire career and had three seasons with over 200 steals.

14

Scottie Pippen

Dominique Wilkins makes a dramatic leap during a 1986 game between the Atlanta Hawks and Los Angeles Lakers.

The Human Highlight Film

In the 1980s and 1990s, Dominique Wilkins made hoop-rattling dunks so incredible that they were often replayed on television. The French-born Atlanta Hawks superstar put up nearly 25 points per game for a career total of 26,668 points. He was also a good defender near the net. During the 1990–1991 season, Wilkins averaged nine rebounds a game.

15

The All-Purpose Player

A small forward needs to do it all: pass, block, dribble, steal, shoot, and rebound. He must also be very good in the **post**. Whatever the situation calls for, that's what a small forward must be ready to do.

Side to Side

Since a basketball team has five players on the court, there are often more players on one side of the basket than the other. An offensive play may call for more players on the left or the right side of the court. The side with the most defensive players is called the strong side. The one with fewer is the weak side.

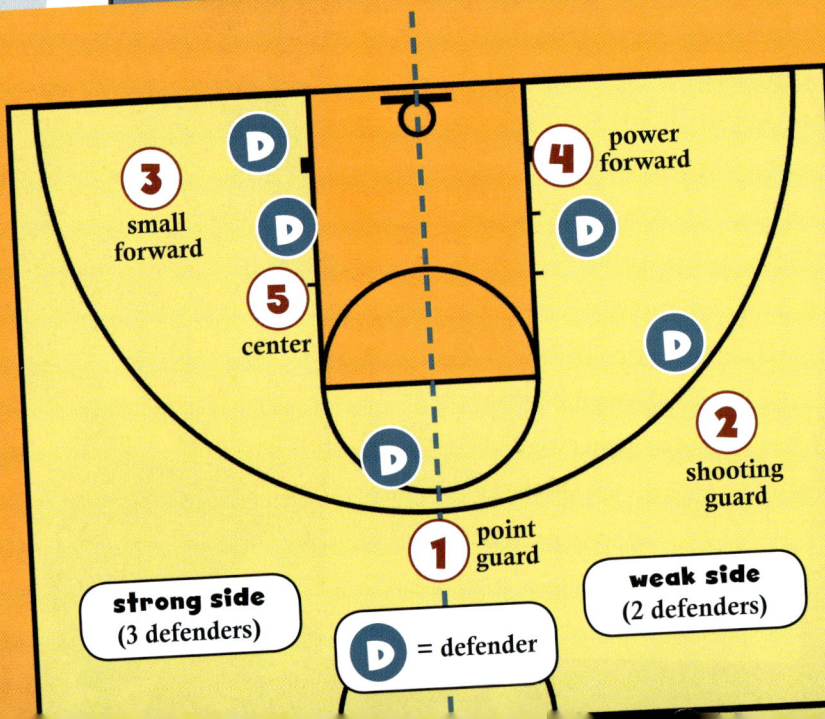

3 small forward

4 power forward

5 center

2 shooting guard

1 point guard

strong side (3 defenders)

weak side (2 defenders)

D = defender

basket

baseline

free-throw lane

wing

free-throw line

wing

three-point line

Where a small forward positions himself on offense depends on what play the coach wants his team to run. The coach may need the small forward close to the free-throw lane or out on the wing. The forwards might line up across the lane from each other. Or they might line up on the same side if the coach runs a "stack" offense.

The Forwards

Basketball teams use two forwards. The power forward is usually taller and stays nearer the basket. The small forward can help close-up, but he's a player who can shoot from anywhere.

17

On Offense

The small forward's job changes from play to play and moment to moment. He has to know the plays and be ready to change roles quickly.

Keep Moving

Small forwards are always on the move to get open. A player can't score or make great passes when he's being blocked by the defense. The defense must always watch a small forward and try to stay between him and the ball.

It's not easy for opponents to stay between the ball and small forward Shawn Marion of the Dallas Mavericks.

18

The Big Screen

If the play doesn't call for the small forward to shoot, it's his job to help a teammate get clear to make a basket. When a teammate makes a move, the small forward should try to position himself in the path of the teammate's defender. If he does well, the defender will have trouble getting around his **screen**, and his teammate will be open to catch a pass and shoot.

Morris Peterson of the New Orleans Hornets protects the ball from his opponent while searching for an open teammate.

19

When the small forward gets the ball, he must read the defense in a flash. If no large defenders are near, it may be a good time to shoot. Forwards with a good jump shot can sink the ball right away. Otherwise, it's time to rush in close before blockers get set.

Elgin Baylor played for the Los Angeles Lakers. Here he's scoring points during a game against the New York Knicks around 1970.

Bank-Shot Baylor

Hall of Fame player Elgin Baylor was one of the best moving shooters of all time. His special play was a "bank shot" off the backboard while crossing in front of the basket. In a bank shot, the ball bounces off the backboard before passing through the hoop. Baylor's bank shot let him get points around and over bigger players.

20

One-on-One

When a small forward is covered, it's usually by just one defender. With or without the ball, a small forward needs to have the ability to get by his defender. By **cutting** inside quickly or faking a move, small forwards should be able to pass a defender to keep the play going.

Toronto Raptor small forward Hedo Turkoglu passes his defender on the way to the basket.

21

Sometimes things don't go as planned during a play. A shot by a teammate can get tipped or can take a wild bounce off the rim. Offensive rebounds give the offense another chance to score. A small forward must be quick enough to get in position for a rebound. Up close, he needs perfect timing to out-jump the defense. If the ball bounces up high off the rim, he needs to be where the ball will come down.

Tip-In

Instead of rebounding the ball, a player with good timing can jump up and nudge it into the basket for an easy two points. This is called a tip-in.

22

Corey Maggette of the Golden State Warriors goes up for a big rebound against the Utah Jazz.

Andres Nocioni of the
Sacramento Kings scores
on a fast break against the
Minnesota Timberwolves.

Running the Court

The small forward should be able to run the length of the court faster than most other players. If the other team steals the ball, the small forward must run to defend the basket. If his team gets the ball and goes on a **fast break**, the small forward must outrun the defenders and be ready for an easy basket.

Key Offensive Skills

No matter what play is called, a small forward must do a few things right every time. Here are a few basics of the small forward's game.

Stand and Deliver

Small forwards need to be able to explode into motion. Having a good stance is the key. A right-handed player usually pushes off with the left foot, so he stands with it slightly behind his right foot. He bends his knees and elbows slightly and squats low, ready to spring. To move side to side better, the feet should be lined up and spread apart with toes pointing out at a slight angle.

In this stance, small forward Luol Deng of the Chicago Bulls is ready to spring into action.

Ball Control

Taller small forwards stay low while they dribble and move from a crouch. If a defender is close, the small forward passes him by edging his head, shoulders, and body past that player with his first steps. The small forward keeps the ball in the hand farthest from the defender. He may need to cross over to the other hand while moving.

LeBron James of the Cleveland Cavaliers controls the ball while driving past his opponent.

The Baseline Cut

Small forwards might run a straight path to the basket along the baseline. If they do, they have to get past defenders and stay inbounds. Cutting in front of defenders makes it possible to receive a pass or screen a defender. If the small forward can make baseline cuts well, he can score easy points as he passes under the basket.

Washington Wizard Caron Butler makes a baseline cut to get in close for a basket.

One of the small forward's primary shots is the **layup**. Here, the forward gets close enough to put the ball in off the backboard. This makes it harder for defenders to block. The layup is simple, but a player needs to demonstrate good ball control to make it work. Missing a layup is a good way to get sent to the bench!

Carmelo Anthony of the Denver Nuggets quickly scores two points off a layup while his opponents watch.

Free Throws

Many of a small forward's points come from free throws due to defenders making illegal contact when the forward goes for a basket. Small forwards practice free throws to make as many as possible.

27

On Defense

The small forward's many skills often make him the team's best defender. Keeping the other team from scoring is as important as scoring points for your team.

Guarding the Player

If a tall player gets the ball directly under the basket, he's likely to score. Small forwards can keep that from happening. On defense, a small forward covering an inside player must stay between his man and the ball. The offensive skills a small forward uses to get past a defender also allow him to cut in front of his man to intercept a pass.

Houston Rockets small forward Shane Battier is very good on defense. Here he rushes in to steal the ball from the opponent.

28

Andre Iguodala of the Philadelphia 76ers keeps his opponent contained on the wing.

Guarding the Ball

If the small forward's opponent already has the ball, the forward must keep the opponent from scoring. The small forward is usually taller than most guards, so he can try to block them while staying ready to shut down a pass or cut. If the other player is taller, the small forward needs to be ready to steal the ball on a high bounce or bad pass.

29

Taking Charge

Offensive players commit fouls, too. If an offensive player runs into a defender who isn't moving, it's called charging. A small forward can make the offense take a charging foul by seeing where a player is going with the ball and getting there first. He must be standing with both feet on the ground before the player with the ball gets there. If the small forward is set and the ball handler bumps him, the offense will get called for charging and have to give up the ball. If the small forward moves or isn't set, he'll get a defensive foul.

It can be hard to avoid fouls when playing defense. Here, Bruce Bowen of the San Antonio Spurs contains his opponent without committing a foul.

Double Up

If the opposing team has a superstar who scores most of that team's points, the small forward might need to work as part of a double-team. A double-team means that two players both cover an opponent when he has the ball. While one player guards against the shot, the other guards against the pass. If the superstar gets a pass away, one teammate continues to defend him, while the other covers an open opponent.

Small forward Brandon Roy (center) and power forward LaMarcus Aldridge of the Portland Trail Blazers double-team Andrea Bargnani of the Toronto Raptors.

31

Before the Game

Quick hands and feet allow a small forward to make plays on the fly. However, being prepared is more important than quickness. Studying and practicing hard gives the small forward the best chance to be in the right place at the right time.

The Long Haul

At the end of a game, when everyone is getting tired, a strong small forward with solid defensive skills is a powerful weapon. Some of the most important training a small forward does involves running and endurance exercises to stay in shape. A tired player is not as fast or accurate and is more likely to foul. Practicing sprints and long-distance jogging helps keep small forwards strong for the whole game.

Utah Jazz small forward Andrei Kirilenko dunks against the Los Angeles Lakers after a fast break late in the game.

It's the small forward's responsibility to work on his weakest skills so he can have a complete game. A good distance shooter should also be good at driving to the basket and rebounding. A great passer should work to become a better dribbler. Mastering as many skills as possible makes the whole team more effective.

Many basketball fans consider Paul Pierce of the Boston Celtics to be the best all-around small forward.

04 Big-Name Small Forwards

Some of the most exciting players in the NBA today are small forwards who play big. Check out a few of the best small forwards in the game today.

King James

The Cleveland Cavaliers **drafted** LeBron James right out of high school, and it may have been the best decision the team ever made. "King James" is the youngest player in NBA history to record a triple-double, score 50 points in a game, average more than 30 points per game in a season, and reach 15,000 career points. He's also an excellent defender and passer. At the pace James is playing, he may become the greatest player of all time.

In April 2010, James won his second NBA MVP award. Only 11 other players have won this award two or more times.

34

Carmelo Anthony helps lead his team to victory over the Dallas Mavericks during a 2009 playoff game.

The "Golden" Nugget

Since Carmelo Anthony joined the Denver Nuggets in 2003, the team has never missed the playoffs. He has also been one of the top 10 scorers in the league every year since the 2005–2006 season. In one game in 2008, he tied a record for most points in one quarter of play with 33 points. While "Melo" can cause problems for the defense up close, he also likes sinking game-winning shots at the buzzer from the outside.

It's no lie that Paul Pierce of the Boston Celtics makes everyone around him better. The man they call "The Truth" is a tough defender who excels at getting the ball to teammates at key times. In 2002, he helped the Celtics make the biggest comeback in playoff history against the New Jersey Nets. The Celtics scored 21 points in the fourth quarter to come from behind and win the game 94–90. The Celtics didn't win the championship that year, but they did in 2008. Pierce was named MVP of the 2008 finals.

Paul Pierce celebrates after scoring two points against the Chicago Bulls during the 2009 playoffs.

During the 2009–2010 season, Durant scored at least 25 points in 29 consecutive games. This is a record among active players.

25 for 35

Kevin Durant of the Oklahoma City Thunder wears number 35, but perhaps 25 would fit him better. That's because Durant is only the third player since 1986 to score at least 25 points in 25 or more consecutive games. Many of those points came from free throws. Durant averages over 400 free throws a season! In 2010, Durant became the youngest scoring champion ever by averaging 30.1 points a game.

Peja Stojaković prepares to score three points during a 2008 playoff game against the Dallas Mavericks.

Three-Point Powerhouse

Peja Stojaković is an unusual small forward because he makes so many points far from the basket rather than up close. The New Orleans Hornet currently has the fourth-highest number of three-pointers in history. Stojaković's also amazingly accurate from the free-throw line, nailing close to 90 percent of his free throws! He's the fourth-most-accurate free-throw shooter in history.

Not so fast! Danny Granger's long arms help him be a big-time blocker.

Big D

Indiana Pacer Danny Granger proves that while talent is good, talent mixed with hard work is better. Granger is the only player in NBA history to improve his points-per-game average by at least five points 3 years in a row. He also works tirelessly to improve his defensive game, and it shows. He's perhaps the best shot-blocking small forward in the league and can often keep larger players from scoring.

39

Future Star: You!

LeBron James became a pro when he was only 18 years old, but he's been sharpening his basketball skills since he was just a toddler. The following drills are good practice for a small forward at any age.

Power Dribbling

Small forwards use power dribbling to move side to side while protecting the ball. Start from a low, crouching stance. Dribble the ball near your back leg, down by your knee or lower. As you dribble, shift your feet from side to side to move forward or back. You should be sliding sideways. Dribble the ball ahead of your back foot to move forward and behind your back foot to go backward.

Take a Seat

A good dribbler looks like he is sitting on an invisible chair. You can actually use the front of a real chair to practice your dribble stance!

Notice how the player with the ball uses her body to protect it from her opponent.

Post Up

Small forwards spend a lot of time in the post, so you should practice your post play. Start with your knees bent and legs wide. With arms up and bent, your hands are held high in front of your face. In this stance, a small forward can use his arms, back, and behind to keep a defender away. Practice catching passes from this position. To get even better pass control, practice catching tennis balls instead.

41

Lay It Up

Layups are easy points for small forwards, so you need to learn them well. The ball starts in your strong hand. Your jump begins from your opposite foot. Bring the other knee up to your chest to lift you up and not forward. Use the rectangle on the backboard as a target. Bounce the ball off the upper corner of the rectangle and into the basket. Once you perfect this, switch hands. Be sure to practice layups on both sides of the net.

Like all shots, layups are perfected with practice.

Rebounding is an important part of a small forward's game and can lead to more scoring opportunities.

Play the Boards

Whether a small forward is on offense or defense, rebounding is your best chance to help your team win. Have a friend take shots while you practice rebounding. Use both feet to get as high as you can. Time the move so you catch the rebound at the top of your jump. Grab the ball with two hands so it can't be knocked away. Land on both feet and hold the ball up beneath your chin with your elbows out to protect it.

Record Book

How do small forwards stand in the NBA record books? Here's an impressive list of numbers the great small forwards have achieved.

LeBron James

Career Points by a Small Forward:

1. Julius Erving	30,026
2. Dominique Wilkins	26,668
3. Alex English	25,613
4. Rick Barry	25,279
5. Adrian Dantley	23,177

Points in a Season by a Small Forward:

1. Rick Barry	2,775	1966–1967
2. Elgin Baylor	2,719	1962–1963
3. Elgin Baylor	2,538	1960–1961
4. Rick Barry	2,518	1971–1972
5. LeBron James (still active)	2,478	2005–2006

Points in a Game by a Small Forward:

1. Dominique Wilkins	57	12/10/1986
2. Glen Rice	56	04/15/1995
3. LeBron James (still active)	55	02/20/2009
4. Dominique Wilkins	54	02/03/1987
5. Dominique Wilkins	53	01/12/1987

Scottie Pippen

Career Steals by a Small Forward:

1. Scottie Pippen   **2,307**
2. Julius Erving   **2,272**
3. Larry Bird   **1,556**
4. Chris Mullin   **1,530**
5. Jerome Kersey   **1,439**

Steals in a Season by a Small Forward:

1. Scottie Pippen   **232**   1994–1995
2. Rick Barry   **228**   1974–1975
3. Billy Cunningham   **216**   1972–1973
4. Steve Mix   **212**   1973–1974
5. Scottie Pippen   **211**   1989–1990

All-Star Game Appearances by a Small Forward:

1. Larry Bird   **12**
2. Elgin Baylor   **11**
   Julius Erving   **11**
4. Paul Arizin   **10**
5. Dominique Wilkins   **9**

45

Glossary

ABA: American Basketball Association, a professional basketball league that existed from 1967 to 1976

baseline: the line behind the basket that marks the end of the court

cut: a sudden run across the floor to get free from a defender

defense: the team trying to stop the other team from scoring

draft: to select from a group of players who have applied to enter a league

dunk: to throw the basketball into the basket from above the rim

fast break: when a team gets the ball back on defense and takes it quickly back the other way for a shot up close against few defenders

foul: a penalty called for breaking rules, usually coming from illegal contact between players

free throw: a chance to shoot for one point after being fouled; the shot is made from a line in front of the basket with no defenders

free-throw lane: the area beneath the basket marked by lines running from the free-throw line to the boundary line behind the basket

intercept: to catch a ball that was being passed from one member of the opposing team to another

layup: a shot made from beneath the basket by bouncing the ball off the backboard and into the net

NBA: National Basketball Association, the men's professional basketball league in the United States; the NBA also includes the Toronto (Canada) Raptors

NCAA: National Collegiate Athletic Association, the organization that controls college sports

offense: the team trying to score

opponent: the person or team you must beat to win a game

post: the area under the basket, also known as the free-throw lane

rebound: a ball recovered off a missed shot

screen: a play where a player moves to block a defender to give a teammate a chance to get open for a pass

steal: a ball taken away from an opponent's control

triple-double: getting 10 or more of three of the following in a single game: points, assists, blocks, steals, or rebounds

turnover: when a team loses control of the ball to the opponent

For More Information

Books

Doeden, Matt. *The World's Greatest Basketball Players*. Mankato, MN: Capstone Press, 2010.

Lupica, Mike. *Long Shot: A Comeback Kids Novel*. New York, NY: Philomel Books/Walden Media, 2008.

Rud, Jeff. *In the Paint*. Victoria, BC, Canada: Orca Book Publishers, 2005.

Schaller, Bob, and Dave Harnish. *The Everything Kids' Basketball Book*. Avon, MA: Adams Media, 2009.

Slade, Suzanne. *Basketball: How It Works*. Mankato, MN: Capstone Press, 2010.

Web Sites

www.hoophall.com
Learn about the history of basketball at the online version of the Naismith Memorial Basketball Hall of Fame. Read the biographies of the greatest basketball players of all time.

www.nba.com
The official Web site of the National Basketball Association has information about teams and players both current and historic. Fans can see videos, get news, check scores, and look over game or season statistics.

www.nba.com/kids
The NBA's official Web site for kids lets you play games, join fan clubs for your favorite team, and learn exercises to make you a better basketball player.

www.sikids.com/basketball/nba
The *Sports Illustrated* Web page for kids lets you follow your favorite NBA team. On this site, you'll find scores and news updates about your favorite sport.

Index

About the Author

Jason Glaser is a freelance writer and stay-at-home father living in Mankato, Minnesota. He has written over fifty nonfiction books for children, including books on sports stars such as Tim Duncan. When he isn't listening to sports radio or writing, Jason likes to play volleyball and put idealized versions of himself into sports video games.